Disney's Beauty and the Beast
The Enchanted Christmas

Adapted by Margo Lundell
Illustrated by Alan Nowell

Based on Disney's *Beauty and the Beast: The Enchanted Christmas* produced by Walt Disney Television Animation. Written by Flip Kobler & Cindy Marcus and Bill Motz & Bob Roth.

A GOLDEN BOOK • NEW YORK
Golden Books Publishing Company, Inc., New York, New York 10106

 Library of Congress Catalog Card Number: 97-71691
ISBN: 0-307-12974-8
A MCMXCVII

The castle was brimming with the music and laughter of Christmas. Chip giggled and ran over to put an ornament on the beautiful holiday tree.

"It's good to see the boy having a proper Christmas. Not like last year!" said Lumiere.

"Momma, please tell the story of last Christmas," Chip begged.

As Chip and the crowd gathered around Mrs. Potts, she began, "Well, let's see . . . Belle had been at the castle for quite a little while. We were beginning to hope that she would be the one to break the spell, but time was running out. So somehow we got the Beast and Belle to ice-skate together the day before Christmas. . . ."

All the servants watched as Belle taught the Beast how to ice-skate.

"One-two-three. Now you try it," Belle instructed.

The Beast actually began to have some fun as he carefully moved across the ice.

Inside the castle, Forte, the organ, was playing his opera when suddenly he heard laughter from outside.

"Have a look, will you?" he asked his sidekick, Fife, the piccolo. When Fife told him that Belle and the Beast were skating together, Forte was furious. If the Beast fell in love and found happiness, he would no longer want Forte as his confidant. "Fife, see to it that this blossoming love wilts on the stem!" he demanded.

In no time, Fife was out on the pond. He grabbed on to the Beast's cape, causing the Beast and Belle to tumble into a snowbank. Belle just laughed as she began to make a snow angel.

But the Beast was horrified when he saw his shape in the snow. "It's the shadow of a . . . monster!" he shouted, and stormed off.

Back inside the gloomy castle, Belle began to make plans to celebrate Christmas, despite the Beast's wishes. The Beast had forbidden Christmas—it reminded him of the day a curse had been placed upon him and the entire castle. But Belle was determined, so Lumiere led her to the attic to find ornaments.

"This is Angelique," said Lumiere, introducing Belle to a lovely angel ornament. "Angelique is the castle decorator."

"You mean *was* the castle decorator," said Angelique sadly. She wanted to help Belle get ready for Christmas, but she was sure the Beast would put a stop to it.

When Forte told the Master about Belle's plans, the enraged Beast stormed through the castle until he found Belle in the furnace room. She had just selected a Yule log for Christmas day.

"There will be no Christmas!" the Beast shouted as he grabbed the log from Belle's hands.

Belle refused to give up so she convinced the servants to help her prepare for Christmas. They all bustled about, decorating the castle. The aroma of delicious food soon filled the air.

In his chambers, the Beast found a present from Belle labeled Do Not Open Until Christmas. The sight of the gift warmed his heart so much that the Beast asked Forte to compose a song for Belle.

"And make it happy!" the Beast added.

Forte nearly burst his organ pipes in anger. He felt that Belle was pulling the Beast away from him. He had to stop her!

When Forte found out that Belle and Chip were searching the castle grounds for a Christmas tree, his plan was hatched. The Beast had forbidden Belle to leave the castle grounds, so that was exactly what Forte convinced her to do.

"In the Black Forest you will find a tree better than any you can dream of," he advised Belle and Chip. "And the tree was always the Master's favorite part of Christmas."

So Belle and the others traveled into the Black Forest.

That evening the Beast wanted Belle to hear his new song. When Mrs. Potts told him that Belle was missing, he became furious.

The Beast looked into his magic mirror to find Belle and saw her leaving in a sleigh. "She promised she wouldn't leave!" he shouted.

While the Beast hurried to the Black Forest, Belle and Chip finally located the perfect tree. As they began to pull their tree across the frozen river, Fife, who had secretly followed them, suddenly whistled. Phillipe, the horse, reared in fear, and Chip fell through a crack in the ice.

Belle reached into the freezing water and managed to rescue Chip. But then she fell in and the current carried her under the ice.

Just when it looked as if Belle would be lost forever, the Beast appeared and pulled her to safety.

By the time they all returned to the castle, it was midnight—Christmas at last.

The Beast was so furious with Belle that he locked her in the dungeon and then retreated alone to his chambers. There, he noticed Belle's gift, and in spite of his anger, he opened it. Belle had given him a storybook about an unhappy prince who learned about Christmas, and love.

The Beast's heart filled with hope. "Maybe it's not too late!" he shouted. He raced to the dungeon and found Belle and the servants singing Christmas carols.

"Belle, can you ever forgive me?" pleaded the Beast.

"Of course," she said quietly. "Merry Christmas."

When Forte heard the Beast go down to the dungeon, he began to play very loudly. The castle began to crumble from the force of his music.

The Beast burst out of the dungeon and ran to Forte's chamber with Belle and the others right behind him.

“Forte, enough!” the Beast shouted as he tore the keyboard off the organ. In a rage, Forte ripped himself from the wall and fell to the floor. Then all was silent. . . .

"Well, the Beast agreed to give Belle the Christmas she'd always wanted," said Mrs. Potts.

"Soon after, the Beast and Belle fell in love, and the spell was broken. And now we can have another joyous Christmas."

Just as Mrs. Potts finished the story, Fife's music filled the air. The Prince and Belle began to dance.

It was turning into another merry Christmas at the castle.